Haunted Places of Europe

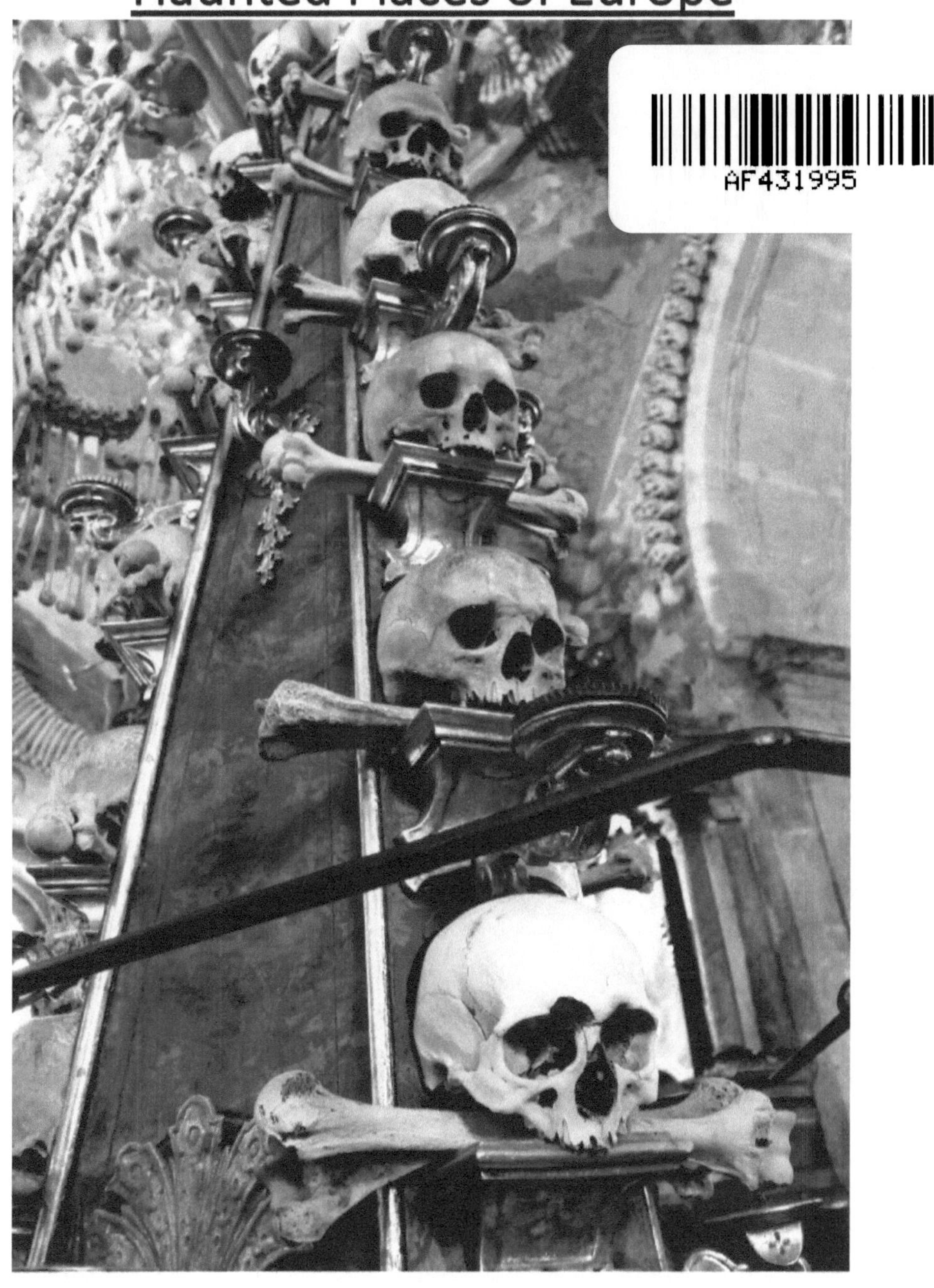

Contents

England

The country of England is chalk full of haunted locations. Some are famous and well known, while others are more obscure. It is not surprising that this island nation is so haunted given the length of the history and human occupation of England. This history includes countless wars, several plagues and plenty of time for a myriad of tragic accidents to occur. There is a cemetery with a resident vampire, haunted bed and breakfasts, haunted pubs and even the ghosts of children. Among the usual tourist sights, here are some of the more paranormal sights for a traveler to add to their list. Don't always trust your eyes though, some people you might meet could have died centuries ago.

The Highgate Cemetery

Located north of the Camden region of London and east of the Hampstead Heath park is the Highgate Cemetery. Opened in 1839, the Highgate Cemetery is the final resting place of some very notable people from George Michael to Karl Marx. According to the information booklet provided by the cemetery when you pay entrance fee, the cemetery began to decline in the 1970s. After the creation of the Charity called The Friends of the Highgate Cemetery Trust, the cemetery began a major rebound. Through their work, over seventy monuments, The Egyptian Avenue, Terrace Catacomb and the Circle of Lebanon are recognized by the English Heritage as historical monuments. However, many people in the area are not convinced that all those interned in the Highgate Cemetery are fully at rest.

One of the major supernatural figures of the Highgate Cemetery is known as the Highgate Vampire. The vampire of the Highgate Cemetery was thought to have originated from a Romanian nobleman and black magic practitioner who was transported to the Highgate Cemetery in a coffin and later resurrected by Satanists.[1][2] One of the first people to see the Highgate Vampire was in 1969 by a man called David

Farrant who is the head of the British Psychic and Occult Society.[1] Farrant described the being as a tall dark entity with entrancing eyes, menacing demeanor and that it had produced an inexplicable chill in the air surrounding him.[2] This sighting, along with the reports of Satanic groups engaging in ritualistic animal sacrifice and black magic rituals had drawn a significant amount of media attention.[2]

Among the tails of the Satanic rituals there were also several graves that were desecrated by the supposed Highgate Vampire and in 1970 a burned, headless female corpse was found near the Cemetery.[1][3] These eerie occurrences only provided credence and justification for the Highgate Vampire legend. The whole situation was going to come to head at some point with amateur vampire hunters and occultists desecrating bodies with one body even being placed in the driver's seat of a car belonging to a person who lived near the cemetery.[3]

The hysteria generated by the Highgate Vampire stories in the media had drawn the attention of a self-described Bishop and vampire hunter called Sean Manchester.[2] According to Manchester the Highgate Vampire was a "king vampire" and gave rise to the tale of the Wallachian (Romanian) nobleman who had been raised from the dead by English black magic practitioners.[2] Manchester and Farrant engaged in a sort of competition on who would slay the vampire first.[2] Manchester ended up declaring there would be a vampire hunt on Friday the 13th in March 1970 which became somewhat of a riot.[3] There were people jumping the cemetery gates, despite the police efforts to prevent this.[3] This event drew large numbers of cameras, fellow 'vampire hunters' and amateur occultists.[2] To the dismay of many, this major vampire hunt was fruitless and the insanity generated was a likely driver for the creation of the Friends of the Highgate Cemetery Charity.

With the advent of the Friends of the Highgate Cemetery group and their restoration work, much of the supposed paranormal activity reports began to decrease.[4] And currently the cemetery is being improved upon daily with an informative visitor's center, guided tours of the west side of the cemetery. During my visit to the Highgate Cemetery I didn't have a spooky encounter or any feelings of dread or terror. However, I did get a feeling of the mourning and the latent emotion of those who have passed as well as those who lost the people they loved. Many of the headstones were engraved with messages and poems that would shake a tear from the foundation of even the most calloused individuals. There were also humorous headstones as well as the absurd amount of attention and reverence paid to headstones of figures such as Karl Marx. Ultimately, wandering the Highgate Cemetery was an emotional experience for me because it was a reminder of the family I have lost. I was mesmerized by the absolute beauty of the monuments/headstones. Any traveler in London should put the Highgate Cemetery on their list of places to visit. Bring a tissue though.

The Black Horse: The Most Haunted Pub in Kent

When it comes to authentic English pubs, The Black Horse is a hard place to beat. Built in 1470 as a farmhouse for a wealthy family that owned much of the area at the time, The Black Horse is situated as a sort of center-piece of the village of Pluckley.[5] Originally The Black Horse was complete with a moat and currently The Black Horse is taking advantage of the agricultural nature of the region by using local produce for the meals that they prepare.[5] The building is absolutely stunning with much of the original woodwork and five fire places to make this restaurant/pub an unbelievably welcoming establishment. Although, the elegance and atmosphere of The Black Horse is probably a good reason why the spirits have yet to leave the pub.

Some tales say that the spirit of the child is a little girl called Jessie. During my visit the bartender told me that spirit of the child mainly bothers the people working in the kitchen and can even be heard laughing at times. The bartender even told me of an instance where a section of exhaust vent in the kitchen was randomly tossed when it was securely fastened and would have been very hard to remove in such a manner.

Other sources say Jessie is an adult woman who is looking for the child she lost.[6]

The other spirits have been said to harass workers who enter the cellar to grab more libations, often physically assaulting them. Cold spots can also be felt in the cellar in a very sporadic manner. There are also reports of an older gentleman who has yet to leave his favorite seat and is still accompanied by his loyal dog. Having a personal bond with my dog and loving The Black Horse I felt this would be the ideal afterlife. Lastly there are the reports of an entity lingering in the upper rooms of The Black Horse. Workers have seen a person through the windows that they didn't recognize and then found out that no one was inside the building. This entity is often reported as a female in a red dress (real British ghost, 2008). Occasionally workers sleep in the upper rooms and have seen the specter of a person as well as having had items moved without explanation. Lastly dogs are said to not dare go up into those rooms.[7]

My visit to The Black Horse was exceptionally strange. I had found the village of Pluckley completely by random while trying to find a place to camp for the night. Since the village of Pluckley is in a rural area, there was plenty of fields and woods to pitch a tent for the night. I turned down one of the few streets in the village and saw a sign that read "the most haunted pub in Kent." That was enough to convince me to go in for a drink. Inside I met some of the most wonderful people and have never felt so welcomed in my life. I made some great friends and the whole experience has given Pluckley a special place in my heart but that's a topic for another day. Hopefully these friends aren't actually ghosts.

<u>The Church of Saint Nicholas</u>

Similar to The Highgate Cemetery, The Church of Saint

Nicholas in the village of Pluckley is also a Grade 1 site as

listed by English Heritage.[8] The Church of Saint Nicholas is

an exquisite looking church, built over 900 years ago. The

Church of Saint Nicholas has an eerie looking cemetery on

the churches hallowed grounds. Having been a staple of the

village and likely a centerpiece of the community, The Church of Saint Nicholas still fills that role today. There are still

regular services held there as well as weddings and funeral

services. While I was in the village the church was undergoing

maintenance to the exterior and the village website states

that they have recently gotten a new organ. Due to this

construction, I did not get an opportunity to go inside but I

did tour the cemetery.

Due to the age of the cemetery there is a definite

creep factor depending on what the time and conditions

surround your visit. The main ghost reported at The Church of Saint Nicholas is that of Lady Dering. She is reported to materialize as lady in red or white clothing.[7] The ghost of Lady Dering is also believed to be responsible for the flickering of lights within the church as well as banging noises that have no explainable source.[7] Some of the stories regarding Lady Dering are inconsistent but all the tales reflect an element of vanity that is not uncommon for the wealthy. In some reports Lady Dering was buried in three coffins, in other reports she is buried in seven coffins.[6][7] Both reports claim this was done in effort to protect her body from the elements that cause decay.

<u>The Dering Arms</u>

"Where the murderers killed each other." This is how The Dering Arms was described to me at first by a bartender at The Black Horse. Granted, when that was the common occurrence at The Dering Arms, the main mode of transport in England was horse-drawn carriage. Built in the 1840's The Dering Arms was used as a hunting lodge, gambling hall and pub. Currently, The Dering Arms is a bed and breakfast on the southern edge of Pluckley and a room goes for about eighty GBP per night. The rooms were relatively spacious and comfortable with an exceptional breakfast. I went out to some of the other pubs in the village and came back to my room "after-hours" and they provided me with a key to the kitchen to get back to my room. I was a bit drunk (or pissed as the English would say) and didn't know where the lights were. I could see my bumping about in the kitchen causing some of the sounds that could be confused with spirit activity.

The majority of the haunting and murderous stories that I heard regarding The Dering Arms were mostly word of mouth tales from the residents of the village. As previously stated, The Dering Arms was the location where the dregs of society would meet, drink and then go to the nearby forest and battle to the death. The forest (yes, the forest near The

Dering Arms is called "the forest") made for a good place to bury the bodies without significant attention being drawn.

Other reports of the hauntings at The Dering Arms are of the odd, ethereal voices and unexplained sounds. There is also a report of an elderly lady who appears in classical garments, wearing a bonnet.[9] This spirit is supposedly so realistic that people mistake her for a real person until she dematerializes when they approach her.[9] I tried to find some evidence of hauntings when I stayed the night there. However, all I had was a peaceful night's sleep. The scariest part of The Dering Arms was a broken toilet in the morning forcing me to go to The Forest to handle some business.

The Dering Woods: AKA The Screaming Woods

The Dering Woods is one of the more well-known haunted locations in the village of Pluckley. Often, The Dering

Woods is described as the most haunted woods in all of England. There are stories of a murderous highwaymen who was dealt justice by a vigilante mob. Disembodied screams and howls emanating from the depths of the forest. An inexplicable Halloween massacre of twenty people. A colonel who took his own life within the forest. Shadow people following hikers and the forest was also the subject of scientific study. Needless to say, The Dering Wood has a very disturbing and strange history. Although, while looking for The Dering Woods, I believe I found an explanation for the screaming sounds.

The Highwayman called Robert Du Bois was a thief and murderer who was well known for ambushing people who were traveling around the area.[7] Robert Du Bois would hide in the hollow of a tree and then pop out and rob folks; if they resisted, he would murder them. Eventually, the villagers had become fed up with Du Bois and his violent crimes and decided to deliver their own brand of justice. The Highwayman's hiding location was discovered and the villagers ambushed the ambush predator.[7] Du Bois was taken to The Dering Woods and pinned to a tree with swords and then beheaded. His spirit is said to still linger in The Dering Woods where he will often spring from behind a tree and give a hiker a ghastly, heart-stopping experience.[10]

In 1948, on the morning of November 1st there was a gruesome discovery of twenty dead people, eleven of which were children, all piled on top of each other.[10] These dead bodies had no external wounds and the initial autopsies were inconclusive, several months later the authorities determined the cause of death was carbon-dioxide poisoning.[10] During the evening in which the murders had to have taken place, there were reports of unearthly lights emanating from The Dering Woods.[10] These lights, the lack of wounds and the seemingly abrupt and quick end of the investigation of the murders gave justification to the people who thought the

massacre was caused by something supernatural.

Military service and experiences of war can have

lasting effects on a person. A soldier's body and a soldier's

mind are very much at risk when subjected to the horrors of

war. Sadly, service members taking their own lives is not only

a modern problem but a historic problem as well. Deep

within The Dering Woods a disheveled army colonel tied a

rope into a noose and then secured it to a tree. After concluding that suicide was the only way out, he put his head through the noose and gave in to death's embrace. Currently the Colonel is seen marching through the forest, walking around with a melancholic expression, sometimes he is seen hanging from the tree and occasionally he is reported to sneak up behind people.[11]

When I went wondering through the Dering Wood I didn't experience much out of the ordinary. The area was rather pleasant and there were plenty of locals walking their dogs and enjoying a stroll through the forest. There were areas that looked very dark since the forests canopy was thick enough to block out a large percentage of the light. I could see how this darkness could get someone spooked if they entered the forest with the idea of hauntings, ghosts and ghouls already in their mind. There were two major things that concerned me about the forest which was the volume of litter scattered around the forest and the signs forbidding camping and anti-social behavior. Pluckley is an absolutely lovely area and the Dering Wood is a beautiful place. Seeing this disregard and lack of respect for one of my favorite places was the only disturbing aspect of the forest. If you end up in Pluckley please treat the land and the people with respect.

What is behind the screaming? Well, I may have found the source of the eerie phenomena. While looking for The Dering Wood on the maps app on my phone I saw something that highlighted the likely source of the "screaming." To preface this, let me say I have always lived in the rural foothills of the Rocky Mountains of Colorado and have been exposed the frightening sounds that wild cats like Mountain Lions and Lynx make. When I saw the Big Cat Animal Sanctuary on the map less than three miles from The Dering Wood I thought "mystery solved." Big cats (not the domesticated kind) make sounds that could easily be described as inhuman/ghastly screaming and these sounds can easily travel the sub-three-mile distance when there is no significant human development to block the sound waves. There is the source of the screaming inhuman entities in The Dering Wood.

Brighton

The city of Brighton on the southern coast of England is an energetic and vibrant place. The pier area is a bustling hub for tourists and events. Brighton also has its fair share of haunted locations to offset the beauty of the city and lovely demeanor of the Brighton inhabitants. Brighton is supposedly one of the most haunted cities in England and there is no shortage of haunted locations here. Most of these locations can easily be viewed on one of the many ghost walks that are offered in Brighton. The ghost walks are well worth your time if you make it to Brighton. Here is a short list of haunted locations in Brighton and some of the stories behind them.

Constable Henry Solomon was the police chief in Brighton until 1844.[12] His time as the police chief was cut short when a man by the name of Lawrence walked into Solomon's office, gabbed a fire poker and beat Solomon to death with it.[12] Henry Solomon's ghost is reported to haunt the building he was killed in. That building is now the Brighton Town Hall. His ghost is reported to be seen outside of the door to his office, on the side of the town hall building.

The Marlborough Pub and Theater is a great classic pub to stop into for a drink. This pub is only a short walked from the famed Brighton Pier and feels more like an old west saloon than an English pub.

However, a couple hundred years ago the owner of the building shoved his wife down the stairs in an attempt to take her life.[13] She survived the initial attack so her husband locked her away in the pub's cellar.[13] His wife laid on the cellar floor, alone, and eventually died from her wounds.[13] Now her spirit is said to be the cause of many of ghastly disturbances that occur in the cellar and on the stairs. If you stop in for a drink at the Marlborough Pub and Theater and hear a weird noise on the stairs or basement, she's trying to get your attention.

Haunted roads are not as uncommon as most people would think. Since many people worldwide die in auto accidents, it is no wonder some roads have lingering spirits. The Hangleton Road in Brighton is supposed to be haunted but these are ghosts from the past rather than spirits of those who died in auto accidents. In the past in Brighton, the Hangleton area was where the majority capital punishments were conducted.[13] This area was home to gallows of the region and when someone was hanged, their body would remain there on display to serve as a warning for everyone else.[13] Corpses on display would be preyed upon by the ravens and crows and there is still an abnormal number of these birds in the Hangleton area.[13] At night people often report seeing the executioner of Hangleton walking along the

Hangleton road, noose in hand and the executioner's hood atop his head.[13]

One of the causes of the large number of reported hauntings in Brighton is where it is located. Being so close to the English Channel, German bombers in WWII would drop their unused bombs on Brighton to conserve fuel for the flight home. As you would expect, this nasty habit killed a vast number of civilians who were just going about their day to day lives. A theatre called the Odeon was bombed while a group of children were seeing a film and everyone was killed.[13] The Brighton Library is built where this theatre used to stand.[13] It is not uncommon to see the ghosts of children in the area. A boy in tattered pajamas carrying his wooden train, trying to find his way home is the most commonly sighted spirit here.[13]

<u>Czech Republic</u>

The Czech Republic is the gateway from Western Europe to some of the lesser traveled European countries. The Czech Republic is a glorious land of mystery and adventure with a rich history and many wonderful sights that any traveler would revel in. For the paranormal enthusiast, the Czech Republic has so many terrifying sights that will leave you unable to sleep at night. There is a castle covering the gate to hell, the assassination site of a major SS officer and even a bridge full of malevolent ghosts. Sit back and enjoy this collection of macabre sites located in the beautiful nation of the Czech Republic.

<u>The Houska Castle</u>

The Houska Castle is quite possibly the most mystifying castle in Europe. Visually, the Houska Castle is not very attractive but its outward appearance is just the beginning of the oddity that is the Houska Castle. Most castles have two major features, fortifications for protection and an advantageous location. The Houska Castle has neither. Fortifications on castles are used to keep out invaders but the Houska Castle is designed strictly to keep things in. The Houska Castle is also in an out of the way location, far from any trade routes. During the time of construction, building the Houska Castle was a massive undertaking for a seemingly low reward. The mystery deepens when you begin to ponder what exactly the Houska Castle was meant to retain within its walls.

Prior to the construction of the Houska Castle, this region of Bohemia was said to be besieged by nightmarish creatures, unholy abominations and human/animal

hybrids.[14]

These supernatural creatures terrorized the peasantry,

destroyed their crops and preyed upon their livestock. The

source was found to be a hole with no visible bottom in the

hills that the monsters were emerging from.[14] At this point,

king Ottokar II of Bohemia ordered the Houska Castle to be

built to contain the demonic infestation.[15] When the Houska

Castle was originally finished, there were no wells for water, no kitchen and no plans for human occupation at all. This castle was strictly a prison for inhuman entities.

During the construction of the castle there was an inmate who was condemned to die for his crimes and the local lord offered him a pardon if he agreed to be lowered into the hole and report back what he had seen.[14] Shortly after being lowered into the hole, the prisoner started screaming in a panic.[14] Once the prisoner was raised from the hole, his hair had turned white, his face had become wrinkled and he was said to have aged 30 years.[14] He recounted seeing hell itself. The hole was promptly covered with the floor of the castle's chapel where the walls are scrawled with Christian scripture, images and incantations. Once the hole was covered, the demonic harassment of the peasantry in the region had ceased. Peace had finally returned to this section of Bohemia.

The Houska Castle had transferred into the hands of the local nobility throughout the years and in the late 1500s it had become a proper noble residence.[15] Eventually, the Houska Castle had gone unused and began to dilapidate.[15]

Renovations on the failing castle began in 1823 and in 1897 it was purchased by princess Hohenlohe who lived in the castle until it was bought by Josef Simonek, the president of the Skoda region.[15] During the occupation of Czechoslovakia by the Nazis, the Houska Castle was annexed and used by the Germans to conduct abhorrent experiments on the locals as well as prisoners of war.[14]

There is no doubt that the Houska Castle is a frightening location filled with terrible history. However, this history is what makes it an interesting location for the adventurous traveler. Getting to the Houska Castle can be a difficult task since there is a lack of public transportation to the region. The easiest way to get to the Houska Castle is to hire a car and drive yourself there or ride a bicycle like I did. It can be made into a day trip if you have a car since it is only 30 or so miles north of Prague. Cell service is spotty near the castle but there is appropriate signage guiding you to the castle. Don't get caught near the castle after dark as there is still reports of monsters on the prowl near the castle once the sun finally sets.

The Sedlec Ossuary

The Sedlec Ossuary, or as it is colloquially known, the Bone Church, is a small Roman Catholic church located in the Sedlec suburb of Kutna Hora, Czech Republic. From the outside, the Sedlec Ossuary is an unassuming central European church. Once inside, the nature of this church radically transforms. As you enter the church you are instantly greeted with a myriad of sculptures made of human bones. Walking down the stairs leads to the large main room where the sculptures get larger, more elaborate and more grotesque. All of this leads a traveler to wonder why the people of Kutna Hora decided put their dead on display in such a macabre house of worship.

In the latter part of the 1270s, the abbot of the monastery in Sedlec traveled to Jerusalem and returned with some soil he had collected from the site of Jesus Christ's crucifixion.[16] This soil was spread over the cemetery of the abbey located where the Sedlec Ossuary now sits.[16] As the word of this consecration spread, this cemetery became a very popular burial location for the faithful in Central Europe. The Hussite wars were followed by the devastating Black Plague which caused a massive influx in burials at the abbey's cemetery.[16] Early in the 15th century a church was built to replace the abbey and they decided the best place to build was in the center of the cemetery.[16] The lower level of the new church was designated as a chapel/ossuary (room where bones are stored) for the large number of people who were exhumed from mass graves during the construction of the church.

Early in the 1500's a nearly blind monk was tasked with

sorting and stacking the skeletons and bones that were being

exhumed.[16] Three hundred years later, a famous Czech

woodcarver was hired to turn the large bone heaps into

something a little more pleasing to the eye.[17] As pleasing to

the eye as human bones could possibly get. Each corner of

the ossuary has a large mound of bones with skulls displayed

on a ledge in front of the mounds. There is a chandelier of

sorts in the center that supposedly has one of every bone in the human body. A cherub under the chandelier is playing a trumpet while holding a skull. There is a display case of the skulls of men who died of head wounds in the Hussite wars. Injuries to these skulls are obvious. There is even a crest of the family that hired the woodworker made from the bones and it is prominently displayed on one of the walls. This crest even features a raven picking (imaginary) flesh off the severed head of a Turkish solider.

With around 50,000 to 70,000 human skeletons on display in the Sedlec Ossuary it is not hard to imagine some of the spirits of the dead are still lingering here.[17] Some of these old churches are spooky enough without thousands of skeletons staring directly into your soul. The macabre displays in the Sedlec Ossuary are truly unique and they are worth going to see. Kutna Hora is only a short train or bus ride from Prague and Kutna Hora is arguably a better vacation destination than Prague. Many hostels and hotels in Prague have information on direct tours to the Sedlec Ossuary so there is little reason to not go see it. Try and listen when you go and maybe you'll hear the dead speak to you, saying "our bones are here and for yours, we await."

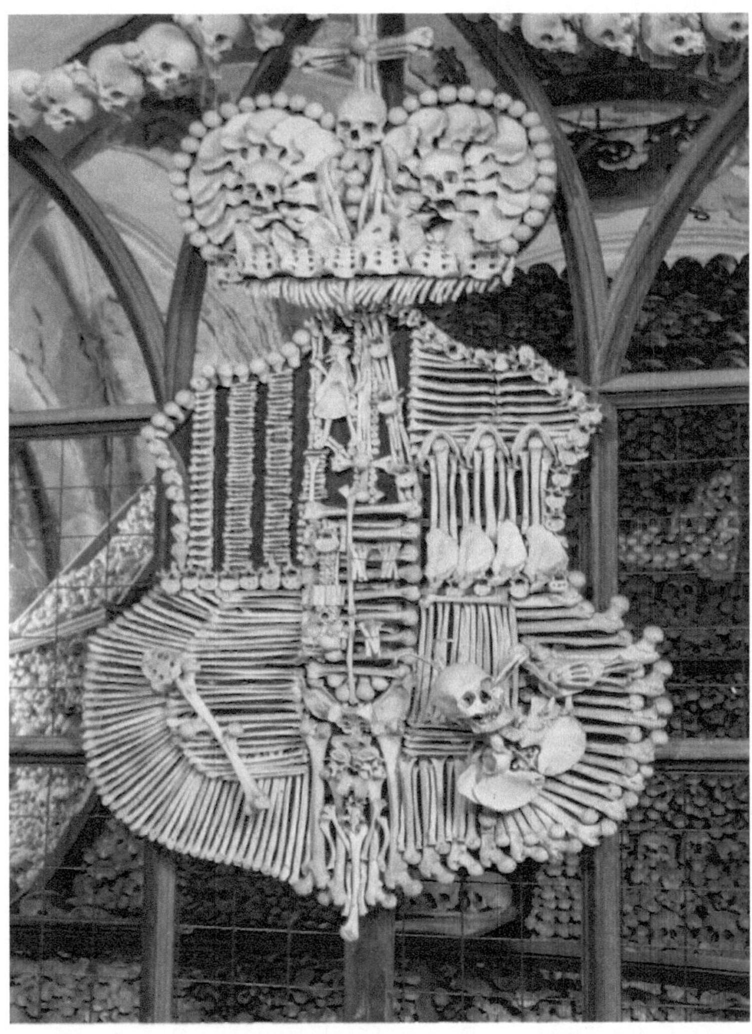

The Church of Saints Cyril and Methodius

Reinhard Heydrich was an absolute butcher of a German SS officer. As the chief of the Reich Main Security Office and the Deputy Reich-Protector of Bohemia and Moravia he was tasked with destroying the Nazi opposition in Czechoslovakia.[18] His tactics for destroying this opposition to the Reich was to try and replace Czech culture and executing the members of the Czech resistance. Hence, he was known by the Czechoslovakians as the Hangman of Prague.[18] His attitude to the Czech people can be summed up in the quote, "we will Germanize the Czech vermin."[18] Heydrich was so confident in the power he wielded over the Czechs that he often drove around alone with his convertible top down. This was a weakness that the Czech resistance movement could capitalize on. Operation Anthropoid was being crafted and the objective was to assassinate the Hangman of Prague.[19]

Frantisek Moravec, leader of the Czechoslovak intelligence services with the approval of Edvard Benes, the exiled head of the Czechoslovak government began planning Operation Anthropoid in 1941.[19] Out of the 2,000 exiled Czech soldiers in Britain, Moravec selected 24 for the mission and they started training in Scotland in October 1941.[19]

After training, the soldiers were transported to the city of Pilsen to meet their allies and then move into to Prague.[19] Many of the Czech resistance fighters wanted the exiled Czech government officials to call off the assassination, arguing that Heydrich's death would have little benefit but extreme consequences for the Czechoslovakian people.[19] Those trying to prevent Operation Anthropoid were correct but their pleas fell on deaf ears.

On the morning of the 27th of May in 1942, two Czech soldiers near the Bulovka Hospital laid in wait for Heydrich's Mercedes.[19] When Heydrich slowed to take a corner, one of the soldiers stepped out in front of Heydrich's car and opened fire with a Sten submachine gun. The Czech soldier's assault was cut short as his gun jammed. Seizing the opportunity, Heydrich stood up with his Luger pistol, took aim, and prepared to fire. Before Heydrich could hit his target, the other Czech soldier tossed a briefcase that contained an anti-tank grenade into the Mercedes with a retracted roof.[19] The anti-tank grenade exploded and injured Heydrich and the Czech soldiers but didn't kill Heydrich immediately. During the chaos, the two Czech soldiers shot at Heydrich with their .32 caliber handguns but all the shots missed. Heydrich returned fire but missed because he was dazed from the explosion. The Czech soldiers had to escape. Heydrich's wounds were ultimately fatal but it took him several months to die.[19]

Hitler was very upset by this act of defiance and came down on the Czechoslovakian people harshly. 13,000 people were arrested and 5,000 of them were killed.[19] German intelligence wrongly tied the assassins to the town of Lidice which led to the Lidice massacre of 199 men and 81 children.[19] After the Lidice massacre no information on the assassins had been obtained. Hitler issued a threat that much more blood would spill if the assassins were not turned in.[19] A member of a Czech saboteur group turned himself in and gave up the names of those involved in Operation Anthropoid to try and get the bounty of one million reichsmarks.[19]

Knowing that the soldiers had been betrayed, they hid in the Church of Saints Cyril and Methodius with the Germans hot on their trail. 750 SS troops assaulted the church with rifles, grenades and machine guns.[19] Despite only having small caliber pistols, the Czech soldiers inside the church managed to kill 14 SS troops.[19] The gunfight lasted two hours and by the end, the Czech resistance fighters inside the church were dead. The bishop of the church took responsibility for the actions of the resistance fighters to limit the revenge of the Germans against his parishioners.[19] The SS then executed the bishop, the priests and the other church leaders.[19] The Czechs paid a heavy price for their actions that are evident today by the bullet riddled wall of the church.[19]

The Old Jewish Cemetery

The Old Jewish Cemetery located in Prague is an odd sight to behold with a long history and legend of a Frankenstein style monster lurking within its walls. Since exhuming a body is against the Jewish religion and the city of Prague passed a law that made burying corpses where people lived illegal; bodies in the Old Jewish Cemetery were just stacked. In some places the graves are 12 bodies deep.[20]

However, they aimed to give each person their own

headstone which is why the grave makers are so cramped

together. It is estimated there are approximately 100,000

bodies in the Old Jewish Cemetery with over 12,000

headstones.[20] The first grave is believed to have been dug in

1439 and the last person interred here was in 1787.[20] One of

the more notorious figures buried here is Rabbi Loeb who is

essentially the Czech/Jewish Dr. Frankenstein according to

the legends of him and his creation.[21] The Golem of Prague.

Rabbi Loeb was known to be a valiant defender of the Jewish people in Prague. He was often referred to as "The Exalted One" because of this.[21] In 1580 there was a troubling issue coming to light in Prague. A priest called Taddeush was spreading a rumor accusing the Jews of conducting ritualistic murders in the hopes of directing the public's ire against the Jewish population.[21] When Rabbi Loeb caught wind of this plan he asked god for help with protecting the Jewish community.[21] God answered the Rabbi in his dreams.[21] God's message was obscure and Loeb had to decipher the instructions via Kabbalistic formulas which he did.[21]

The answer delivered to Loeb was to create a Golem from clay, give it life and the Golem will destroy the enemies of the Jewish people.[21] Through some complicated Jewish mystical ritual, Rabbi Loeb brought the Golem to life and it served its purpose of keeping the Jewish community safe.[21] However, the Golem eventually went mad and became a danger to everyone.[21] Luckily, the creation didn't kill the creator before the creator could destroy the creation. The Rabbi eliminated the Golem from this realm of existence.[21] Some legends say that the Golem can still be seen lurking in the darkness, protecting the Old Jewish Cemetery from any who dares enter its walls with ill-intent.

Charles Bridge

The Charles Bridge is one of the most iconic sights in Prague. Given that construction started in 1357, this bridge is a true feat of engineering. However, like many things in Prague, there is always some bizarre history behind the beauty when you look a little deeper. This pedestrian bridge draws tourists from around the world and features some exceptional historical and religious statues. During the day, there are no shortage of merchants, artists and tour groups. However, at night, other entities come to life on the bridge. The Charles Bridge has a long history of being haunted by several ghosts and has even had a visit from the devil himself.

The legend states that King Wenceslas IV decided to dispose of the body of Saint John into the Vltava river by throwing the corpse off the Charles Bridge.[22] That night, an incredible flood hit Prague which knocked down part of the bridge.[22] During the repair process, the freshly repaired parts of the bridge were constantly being washed away in the night. One worker decided to stick around to see if the destruction was caused naturally or by a saboteur.[22] What he saw that night was more terrifying than he could have imagined. The worker who stayed there that night was greeted by Satan and he declared he would continue to destroy the new construction until he took a soul as payment.[22] He was going to take the soul of the first person that stepped on the new sections of the bridge.[22] The worker took this threat seriously and began to guard the bridge. Sadly, the first person that stepped foot on the new section was his pregnant wife who was crossing the bridge to tell him that she was going into labor.[22] During the birthing process his wife died and the child died shortly after.[22] Legend has it that the woman's soul was taken to hell and the child's ghost is commonly seen on the bridge.[22]

Hundreds of years ago, European rulers had a nasty habit of public capital punishment. Often, these public executions included graphic displays to serve as a warning to the rest of the citizenry. Vlad the Imapler is one of the most well-known rulers to practice this, but Czech rulers did similar things. Over the course of 10 years (1621-1631) there were 10 Czech lords who ran afoul of the ruler of that time and lost their heads.[23] Literally. Severed heads of these 10 lords were stuck on pikes and displayed on the Charles Bridge.[23] These 10 lords are known to haunt the Charles Bridge, singing sad songs and attacking the living that look for the source of the singing.[23] If you're walking on the Charles Bridge at night and hear singing, don't go looking for the source of the singing.

On a summer solstice in the early 1600s, twenty-seven noblemen were executed for participating in the revolution against the Habsburg royal family.[24] Three were hanged and the other twenty-four were decapitated with a sword.[24] These severed heads were divided into two groups of twelve and placed into wire baskets.[24] The baskets of unspeakable gore were displayed on the two towers at each end of the Charles Bridge and remained there until all the flesh had rotted away. When the baskets came down, the heads were just skulls. The smell must have been nauseating. I can imagine the angry spirits of these men might be lingering on or near the bridge as well.

Slovakia

Slovakia is located where the hills of Moravia (Czech Republic) turn into the mighty mountains of the Tatras. It is an outdoor adventurer's dream come true! There are alpine lakes that act as massive mirrors, endless hiking trails, and towering peaks reaching well above 2000 meters. The scenery is not the only selling point of Slovakia; the populace is very hospitable and kind. Many who travel the country are hard pressed to come up with any negative words about the locals. However, given the long history of this landlocked nation, there are some horror stories that have occurred within its boarder. Slovakia is home to one of the most famous and evil women in history! Go see Slovakia—your wallet, appreciation of beauty and sense of adventure will thank you.

Hrad Cachtice

Deep in the Slovakian countryside lies the ruins of a castle known as Hrad Cachtice or the Cachtice Castle in English. These ruins are a beautiful testament to the engineering prowess of the Moravians of the 13th century. The Cachtice Castle is built on hill that contains a vast number of rare plant species and is now considered a nature preserve of sorts by the Slovakian government. These ruins are surrounded by a sea of trees and rocky hills but there is a darker reality to this region. In 1575 the ownership of the Cachtice Castle was transferred to its most notorious owner; the Hungarian countess, Elizabeth Bathory.[25]

Elizabeth Bathory is known to most as the Blood Countess and is one of the main progenitors of the vampire legends. Oddly enough, she is related to the infamous Vlad Dracula, cementing this family's reputation of terror. Elizabeth Bathory was born in the Transylvania region of modern day Romania to a very distinguished lineage of nobles,[26] but nobility is hardly correlated with morality. The legends say that Bathory was not only educated on being posh but also educated in Satanism, black magic and torture techniques.[26] When Bathory and her husband moved to Cachtice Castle, she had a personal torture chamber built to her liking.[26] This chamber still stands today.

Elizabeth Bathory is the world record holder when it comes to the number of kills by a female serial killer and the Cachtice Castle was where her victims were slain. She didn't always kill for fun, or to satisfy some animal instinct. She mostly killed for vanity. Elizabeth Bathory thought that bathing in the blood of her young female victims would help her maintain her youthful appearance and peasant girls were not in short supply.[27] Bathory recruited these young women from the surrounding villages with the promise of jobs, lodging in the beautiful Cachtice Castle and teaching them to be proper ladies. What those women got instead was absolute horror. Peasant girls were abused and worked relentlessly until Bathory needed her "beauty treatments." When the time came, the girls were hung upside down, had their throats slashed open and their blood drained into a tub.

Bathing in the blood of these unfortunate women was just one aspect of Elizabeth Bathory's degeneracy. Her other guilty pleasures involved ramming objects under the nails of her victims, smearing girls with food and tying them down outside to be ravaged by insects and subjecting them to the rack.[26] After the death of Bathory's husband, the little remaining shred of sanity she had, fell away. Bathory recruited her personal nurse and a local witch to help ratchet up the brutality.[26] Her vampiric tendencies ramped up to the point that she was biting chunks off the servant girls and even forced one girl to cook and eat her own flesh.[26] Literal bloodbaths increased to the point these women were abducting girls in the night and eventually murdered several daughters of the local nobility.[26]

An estimated 600 women met their end by the hands of Elizabeth Bathory and this greed (plus murdered noble daughters) would be her undoing. Families of the girls sent to the Cachtice Castle began to ask questions, as did the other nobles in the area.[26] Where could so many peasant girls have gone and why did Elizabeth Bathory continuously need more female servants? What was really going on at the Cachtice Castle? King Matthias sent an envoy to the Cachtice Castle to investigate the missing noble women and they reportedly walked into an active torture session.[26] This was the final straw for the nobility above Elizabeth Bathory and she had to be punished.

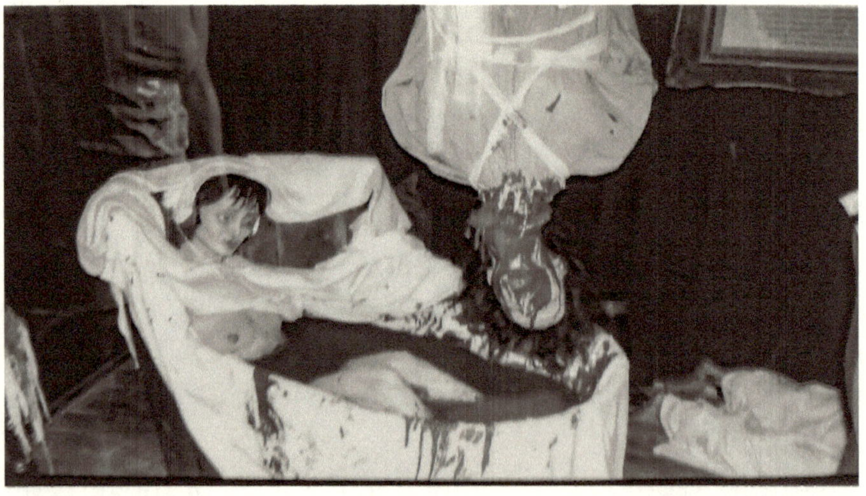

Elizabeth Bathory, her nurse and the witch were all tried for the murders of the girls within the walls of the

Cachtice Castle.[26] Upon conviction, the nurse and witch were promptly executed but Bathory's noble blood saved her from the gallows. Bathory was walled up in the Cachtice Castle with only a small hole for air and food to passed through.[27] She was in there for three years. At one point, she complained to the guard that she was feeling cold, the guard left to retrieve a blanket and when he returned the Blood Countess was dead.

National boarders in this region of Europe have fluctuated significantly over the years and that's why a Hungarian countess had a castle in modern day Slovakia. The Cachtice Castle is an easy day trip from Bratislava. Hop a train from Bratislava to Visnove and not the city of Cachtice. Visnove is much closer to the castle. I took the train to Cachtice and ended up having to walk about six miles each way. Visnove is only fifteen minutes by foot from the castle itself and Visnove is a very eerie village that only adds to the vampiric feeling of the area. Although, try to make time to see the city of Cachtice too because there are many lovely restaurants and lots of local lore surrounding the Cachtice Castle. To ensure your safety, a little garlic around the neck couldn't hurt.

Romania

Romania is one of the more supernatural countries a traveler can step foot in. This Eastern European nation has a long history of paranormal legends and is known to be the origin place of the vampire legends. Originally, Romanian vampires were known as Strigoi before the term vampire entered the global lexicon. Romania has an infamous past ruler that also advanced the legend of vampires thanks to his brutality and an Irish author. As far as a travel destination, Romania should be on everyone's list. Romania has beautiful coastlines, epic mountains, incredible medieval cities and a mass of haunted locations. For people who are interested in the spooky aspects of life, Romania has cursed bridges, a long trail of a Turk impaling national hero, a haunted chemical plant, the worlds most haunted forest and even a cursed monastery. There is something for everyone to love and to be terrified by in the great nation of Romania.

Bridge of Lies

In the heart of one of Romania's most intact medieval cities is quite possibly the world's oldest lie detector device. There is a bridge in Sibiu, Romania that connects the old section of the city to the new section of the city. This bridge is known to the locals as the bridge of lies. However, depending on who you ask, the reasons for this name can be quite different. There are four distinct legends behind the name of this bridge and if you ever end up here you can test some of them out for yourself.

The easiest legend to test without ending up in a Romanian prison is just to tell a lie while on the bridge. If the bridge creaks or moans when you lie, then the most common legend is true. The second legend states that merchants that were found to be crooked or corrupt would be publicly exposed on the bridge, making the whole city aware of their lies.[28] The third legend of the bridge of lies is that people make promises here when they have no intention of keeping them.[28] Lastly, women would tell their fiancés that they were virgins, saving themselves for their future husbands while on the bridge. If these women were found to have lied, they would be thrown from the bridge to the cobblestone street below. Ghosts of some of the women killed by this practice are claimed to linger on the bridge and may be the cause of the noises heard when a lie is told here. Sibiu is beautiful and if you find yourself here (and you should) the bridge of lies is very easy to find.

Poenari Citadel

The Poenari Citadel is Perched on a cliff near the Făgăraş Mountains along the Transfăgărăşan road in Argeş County, Romania. This is the real residence of Vlad Tepes, Vlad III Dracula (the son of the dragon) or Vlad the Impaler as he is more commonly known. Vlad is the man who inspired the character Count Dracula. Although the Poenari Citadel is now abandoned, it was once a glorious stronghold of power for one of Romania's most notorious national heroes. At the Poenari Citadel there was no limit to the cruelty that was dished out at the hands of Vlad Dracula and this castle also has a history of suicide. What more could you ask for in a haunted location? The Poenari Citadel can only be safely seen in an organized tour. The tour starts with a climb up more than 1400 steps with the group being led and trailed by armed guards due to the threat of large brown bears. Some slower visitors may become an easy meal for these animals if not for the guards.

In the mid 1400s Vlad Tepes discovered and developed an affinity for this robust hilltop fortress. Vlad's love for Poenari stemmed from its an advantageous position that could be fashioned into a major stronghold.

Vlad began the task of repairing the Poenari Citadel, eventually making it his home base for ruling over Wallachia. Vlad Dracula was a cruel but effective ruler that impaled those he deemed un-loyal as well as the Turkish invaders. This is what made him a national hero but also contributed to his demise. His temper and habit of impaling people soured some of the relationships that he had with other noble families in the region leading them to turn their backs on Vlad when he was at his lowest.[29]

The walls of Poenari could never be overrun and defeating Vlad Dracula in battle had proven to be an impossible task. The hills surrounding the Poenari Citadel, the hills of Brasov, the general uphill advantage provided by Wallachia made Vlad the ultimate force to be reckoned with. To deal with Vlad, the Turks recruited Vlad's younger brother Radu Bey.[29] Radu was a muslim and Vlad was Christian which allowed the bonds of family to be broken in the quest of power and religious domination.[29] Radu knew where the Poenari Citadel was and began to assault the fortress. During this siege, Vlad's wife committed suicide by jumping off one of the towers of Poenari down to the Argeş river below. She was claimed to have said "I would rather be eaten by the fish than become a captive of the Turks."[29] Unless the rivers flow has shifted, there is no way she made it to the river but rather hit the rocks below.

Radu's assault on the Poenari Citadel had failed initially but it ultimately led to Vlad's downfall. Vlad left the safety of Poenari to attack Radu and his men. However, Vlad had little men remaining in his regiment.[29] Vlad went to the other noble families of Wallachia to ask for money to fund his army of mercenaries but he was denied.[29] When Vlad's remaining legion of loyal men went to attack Radu, he was greatly outnumbered and they lost the battle.[29] While there is no evidence of what happened to Vlad after the battle, legends claim Vlad's head was put on a pike and carried back to Constantinople to prove to the Turkish leaders that the infamous Vlad, the son of the dragon, was finally dead.

<u>Fortress of Targoviste and the Chindia Tower</u>

The city of Targoviste, Romania was once the capital

city of Wallachia and the central political hub of the city was

the Targoviste Fortress. During the reign of Vlad Tepes (Vlad

the Impaler) he ordered the construction of a massive tower

to use as an observation point and storage area for major

valuables of the principality.[30] Vlad's tower was called the Chindia Tower and it became the symbol of Targoviste. As with anything associated with Vlad the Impaler, ghastly stories are common and the bloodshed within this fortress' walls are no exception.

Vlad the Impaler had a long running feud with the Turks and demanded loyalty and obedience from the Wallachian people. Vlad also had a justifiable grudge against the Boyars (elites/nobility of the region) in Targoviste for the murder of his father and one of his brothers in the past.[31] In 1457 Vlad took his revenge against the population of Targoviste by having the Boyars impaled within the walls of the Targoviste fortress as he watched from the Chindia Tower.[31] After the city witnessed their prince impale the Boyars, Vlad had the young people of Targoviste sent to serve him at his main residence, the Poenari Citadel.[31]

Targoviste had seen some other Romanian elite executed 532 years later; it seems Targoviste is where Romanian elites go to die.

In the modern day, the Targoviste Fortress is the main attraction for the city. The Targoviste Fortress is a grand open air museum of sorts with the Chindia Tower, numerous ruins, old churches and even a graveyard. You can walk in the places where Vlad impaled the disloyal Wallachians and stand where he stood while the pikes were raised. Targoviste currently uses these grounds for theater performances, concerts, medieval festivals and even a "Dracula Medieval Festival." Targoviste can easily be seen in a day trip by train from Bucharest and the city is small enough to make intra-city taxis very affordable.

Hoia-Baciu Forest

The Hoia-Baciu forest is well known as the world's

most haunted forest. Located just west of the city of Cluj-

Napoca lies the notorious Hoia-Baciu forest. This forest is 1.9

square miles of mystery with legends ranging from hundreds

of years ago to the modern day. The Hoia-Baciu forest is also known as the Romanian Bermuda Triangle. Most people, myself included, have experienced some very strange occurrences within the forest. The most infamous place in this forest is the unexplained clearing where trees refuse to grow and vegetation is limited when compared to the surrounding region. The paranormal activity in the Hoia-Baciu includes ghosts, poltergeists, UFOs, portals to other dimensions, disappearances and unpleasant physical conditions/electrical disturbances.

The Hoia-Baciu forest's name comes from the name of a shepherd who disappeared with his flock of 200 sheep within the forest.[32] The disappearance of the shepherd and his flock are made more mysterious because of the small size of the forest. It would be impossible to get lost for a long period of time or to die and leave no physical evidence in such a small forest. Another famous paranormal disappearance of the Hoia-Baciu is that of a 5-year-old Romanian girl who vanished without a trace.[33] She emerged years later in the same clothing and she hadn't aged a day despite being gone for several years.[33] Many locals are reported to be afraid to enter the forest, fearing that those who enter will never return home.

People who go into the Hoia-Baciu forest often describe a myriad of odd symptoms ranging from severe anxiety, nausea, panic attacks, headaches, the feeling of being watched, malfunctioning electronics and even skin burns, rashes and scratches.[32][33] Personally, I have experienced an odd metallic taste in my mouth, my drone's remote control turning on while securely in a case in my backpack and camera batteries draining in record time. None of these things had happened before or after, while on the 1,000+ mile bicycle trip that I went on to visit all the locations written about in this book.

The biggest draw and most unexplainable feature of the Hoia-Baciu forest is the mysterious clearing. The clearing is almost a perfect circle with no trees despite large, seemingly healthy trees surrounding the clearing. Within the clearing there are no tree stumps or evidence that the trees have been removed, nor is there evidence that the clearing is maintained, mowed or grazed. Most of the paranormal sightings and occurrences within the Hoia-Baciu occur in this clearing. This is supposedly where the Gypsy witches in Romania meet on their holidays to conduct occult rituals. The fire pits in the clearing are where these rituals are said to be conducted and their holidays are when the veil between the human realm and paranormal realm are thinnest.

In the 1960s Alexandru Sift, a Romanian biologist, started to investigate why the clearing is devoid of trees and why the trees grow crooked within the Hoia-Baciu.[32] His soil sample results were inconclusive; finding no reason why there are abnormalities in the vegetation of the forest.[32] Despite the same species of tree growing normally elsewhere in the region. Everything within the Hoia-Baciu forest is abnormal. This man of science may not have determined why the trees grow in such a manner but he also described many of the same paranormal phenomena that plagues others in the Hoia-Baciu. Paranormal phenomena described by Alexandru Sift includes the feeling of being watched by the shadows and auditory hallucinations featuring the disembodied giggling of female voices, inexplicable rustling, and ethereal teeth chattering.[34]

The Hoia-Baciu forest gained even more notoriety on the world stage in 1968 when a technician in the Romanian military named Emil Barnea produced a compelling photograph of a UFO hovering over the clearing in the forest.[33] This photo has not been found to be doctored. What also makes this sighting is so compelling is that reporting a UFO or paranormal activity in what was an authoritarian, communist country has serious negative impacts. Emil had nothing to gain by releasing this information and everything to lose. In fact, he lost his position during a time when Romania had no safety net for the recently unemployed.[33] In the 1970's, the Hoia-Baciu forest was a hotbed of sightings of UFOs and other unexplained lights.

The most inexplicable paranormal experience that I personally dealt with in the Hoia-Baciu was a time warp or a portal. There are many tales of this phenomena existing within the Hoia-Baciu, these portals are said to be the cause of the many disappearances. On my first nighttime visit to the Hoia-Baciu I met three Romanian people in the clearing.

All of us were a bit frightened by each other but after talking for a few minutes and sharing a smoke we agreed to go explore together. There are several trails leading into the infamous clearing and we just picked one at random to walk down. We walked for quite some time staying slightly to the left and straight. After 30 minutes or so of walking we ended up back in the clearing despite walking away from the clearing. Strangely, we came back into the clearing from an entrance on the right of where we exited but hadn't walked long enough to completely circle the clearing. One of the Romanian men had a GPS device with him. His device showed that we had walked five kilometers in three minutes, despite walking much longer than three minutes. All of us were baffled and terrified, having no explanation for what had just happened.

Ultimately, the mystery of the Hoia-Baciu forest may never be solved. There are so many stories from so many angles. There is everything from ghosts, poltergeists, UFOs, mysterious lights, portals to other dimensions, living shadows and disappearances. The numerous long-told legends and the modern tales of the paranormal will always be a source of interest for the curious travelers in the world. I have had my own weird experiences within the forest that I cannot explain. The legends of the Hoia-Baciu are beginning to rival the legends of Dracula and vampires in Romania and this place of mystery will continue to draw people looking for thrills and proof of life after death for years to come. If you are brave enough to investigate these claims for yourself, just remember, you're never alone in the Hoia-Baciu.

Getting to the Hoia-Baciu forest is quite simple. Cluj-Napoca has an airport and is a major train hub for the region. You can fly into Cluj-Napoca directly or catch a train from Bucharest and make it a several-day trip. Cluj-Napoca is a much nicer vacation destination than Bucharest so spending several days here is far from a burden. There are many bike rental locations in Cluj-Napoca and getting there is an easy ride or you can hop in a taxi. Any taxi driver worth their salt will know where to drop you off. Just don't become one of the damned that never gets to leave the Hoia-Baciu.

Chimopar Chemical Plant

Locations become haunted for various reasons. What happens when you combine the secrecy of an authoritarian government with the production of dangerous military chemicals and numerous deaths? It is quite possible you could end up with a haunted chemical production facility and the Chimopar chemical plant outside of Bucharest is the perfect example. The Chimopar plant itself is a ghost of the past and from the looks of it, the spirits of the dead workers are not well hidden.

When you approach the Chimopar plant the first thing you'll notice is an effluvium of toxic chemicals before you even see the mass of abandoned structures.

(Old Discarded Gas Mask)

This sea of dilapidation looks more like an abandoned city than an amalgamation of factory buildings. Nevertheless, this was a major source of gunpowder and military chemicals for the Romanian government to use for themselves and to export. Given the chemicals produced at Chimopar it is no wonder there was secrecy surrounding it and an inherent danger to the workers. Explosions and accidents were commonplace.

The Chimopar plant was founded in 1895 and specialized in the production of gunpowder and "special chemicals" that I can only imagine were chemical weapons like mustard gas.[35] In 1904 the Chimopar plant was rocked by a massive explosion that claimed the lives of several workers. The sudden nature of death in the explosion can essentially keep the souls of the dead workers on repeat, not knowing they are deceased.[36] In 1923 there was another explosion at the Chimopar plant that claimed the lives of several more workers, condemning them to an eternity of uncertainty.[36] It would be understandable if some of these souls were angered and decided to stick around to harass the living. The most recent accident that claimed the lives of workers was in 1979.[36] However, the secrecy of the times where the communist Romanian government was in power make the information regarding the incidents and casualty figures hard to determine. There is no doubt that the amount of death and misery caused by the events at the Chimopar chemical plant can leave a lasting presence of those who lost their lives there.

In the modern day, the Chimopar plant is still operational but much of the campus now sits abandoned. There are minimal fences to keep people out and seeing other people there is common. Some people that I saw while at Chimopar were scavenging for valuables, spray painting the abandoned structures, feeding the stray dogs, exploring, living within the abandoned buildings and even people filming a music video. The chemical smell is overpowering and will make most people feel ill after a while. I had a distinct feeling of being watched the entire time I was at Chimopar. It may have been human eyes or the eyes of the damned but without a doubt this ghost of the past contains some residual energy of the men who died here and had their deaths concealed by state secrecy.

Visit Chimopar at your own risk and wear boots, it would be very easy to get hurt here. It is worth a visit if you're in Bucharest. To get to the Chimopar Plant you can take the Bucharest subway's M3 line to the Nicolae Teclu stop/station. After that stop, take a short walk on Bulevardul Theodor Pallady, turn when you see the large blue Dedeman building and walk towards the Dedeman entrance until the paved road and fencing stop. You can also take the Bucharest light-rail system to the Chimopar stop, then continue to the

Dedeman building. The Dedeman entrance is on an unnamed street and the accessible part of Chimopar is opposite of Dedeman on the unnamed road.

(*The Dedeman and Unnamed Road Across from Chimopar*)

Execution Site of Nikoli and Elena Ceausescu

Located about a quarter of mile from the train station in Targoviste Romania, is a small but powerful "museum." This is where the Ceausescu couple was tried and executed after the Romania's revolution against communism. I use the word museum loosely because there are only three small rooms and an outdoor area but this is one of the most powerful museums that a traveler can possibly go to. While there are no explicit ghost stories surrounding this museum, it is hard to deny the presence that is felt while on the grounds of the Ceausescu's execution site.

While walking to the door of the building there are signs explaining the history of the events that happened surrounding the revolution in Romania and the last days of the Ceausescus. Once you enter the museum there is an

undeniable heaviness in the air and an eerie silence. Inside

the building, the main room is a beautiful blue with white

inner trim and golden outer trim. Directly to the left of the

entrance door, there is a worker to collect a very small fee.

Directly to the right of the main door is the entrance to

Colonel Andrei Kemeniei's office which was used as a medical

examination room for the Ceausescu couple before their

trial. Directly ahead of the front door is the Documents and Paperwork Office that was used as the room for the trial by the exceptional military court. Down the only hall that is open to the public there is the Chief of Staff's Office that was where the Ceausescu couple was housed for their last four days and three nights. The juxtaposition of the absolute luxury the Ceausescu couple enjoyed in Bucharest and the peasant-like conditions they experienced in their last days is a powerful sight to behold.

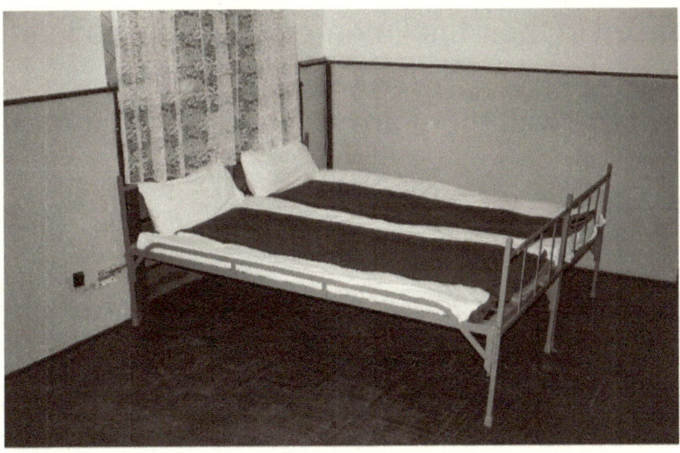

The outside area on the backside of the building is by far the most haunting place in this museum, possibly the legitimately haunted part of the museum as well. A short walk from the door leading outside is the execution site of the Ceausescus. A small section of wall is noticeably different from the rest due to the chunks that have been blown out by projectiles fired from AK-47s. The defined holes beyond the missing chunks of wall where the fatal volley came to rest in the bricks give an insight into the chaos the Ceausescus experienced in their final moments. On the concrete walkway in front of the wall there are also sections that have been pulverized by machinegun fire. Also, there are the chalk-outlines where the Ceausescus bodies' fell after ninety of the powerful 7.62x39mm rounds fired from fully automatic AK-47s ripped through them, bringing their reign to an end.

Chiajna Monastery

The Chiajna Monastery lies on the western outskirts of

Bucharest Romania. While the claims of hauntings are yet to

be proven, the assertion that the Chiajna Monastery is

cursed is demonstrable when looking at the history of the

building. Constructed in the late 1700's, the Chiajna

Monastery was a massive undertaking for the period with its

height nearing 60 feet, a length of 142 feet and walls from 3 to 6 feet thick.[37] The level of strength and security that the monastery was supposed to provide for its faithful congregation was also the catalyst for the monastery's downfall. Given the fortress like appearance of the Chiajna Monastery the Ottoman Turks mistook the house of worship for a military building and besieged the monastery before the building and grounds were properly consecrated.[37] Sadly, for history buffs, the Ottoman Turks destroyed all the documents contained within the monastery. After the chaos of the Ottoman Turks, the faithful Romanians began to try and restore the monastery. However, their troubles were not over.

Shortly after the Chiajna Monastery was being rebuilt after being attacked by the Ottoman Turks, death was again coming to the cursed monastery. This time, death came in the form of plague. Prince Caragea came from Constantinople to rule over Wallachia in late 1812 and shortly after his arrival cases of bubonic plague (the black death) began popping up.[38] Come June of 1813 over 100,000 people countrywide had succumbed to the plague and around 300 people per day were dying in the capital of Bucharest.[38] With the daily sense of dread that was felt among the Romanian population, the restoration efforts of the Chiajna Monastery came to a halt. At this point, all hope was lost and construction on the Chiajna Monastery never resumed.

The mystery surrounding the Chiajna Monastery doesn't end with plagues and invaders, this is where it begins. Around the time of the official abandonment of the

Chiajna Monastery, the monastery's bell was thrown into the Dâmbovița River. Local folks claim that they can hear the bell's toll on nights when the moon is full and on the feast day of the Chiajna Monastery's patron saint John Jacob the Hozevit.[39]

The fires caused by the Ottoman Turks and the subsequent deterioration of the Chiajna Monastery have formed into an auspicious sign that is often referred to as the Romanian Sphinx. Located on the middle of right wall just inside the entrance of the monastery, plaster has become detached and formed in the shape of this Romanian Sphinx.[40] This is called the Romanian Sphinx because of its uncanny resemblance to the Sphinx in Egypt. Others claim this figure is that of an angel or "the lady of Chiajna."

Modern day mysteries of the Chiajna Monastery are the numerous disappearances from the surrounding Giulesti neighborhood, murders on the monastery grounds and living shadows. When walking in the Giulesti neighborhood, especially at the cemetery gates, the Chiajna Monastery can be seen looming over the neighborhood. It is almost as if the monastery is exerting a supernatural force or draw upon the residents and visitors of the area. Many people report massive, dynamic shadows on the walls of the monastery. These shadows move independently of anything between the monastery and the sunlight. There are two recorded, unsolved murders that took place on the Chiajna Monastery grounds around 1990 that are rumored to be the result of the paranormal forces that rule over the cursed monastery.[37]

Ultimately, the Chiajna Monastery is a place of significant mystery and legend. While it may be hard to prove the paranormal claims, it is hard to dispute the claims of this being a cursed monastery. Given the history of the Chiajna Monastery, it is one of the more bizarre cases that I have explored in Romania and it is worth a visit if you're ever in Bucharest. Just go during the normal operating hours lest you become the next case of paranormal murder or disappearance on the grounds of the cursed Chiajna Monastery.

Getting to the Chiajna Monastery can be a little difficult without personal transportation like a bike, car or motorcycle. You can take the train system to the Gara Bucurestii Noi stop and walk up Strada Dumitru Iordan (you can only walk one direction as it ends at the train station).

Once you hit the end of that street turn left and walk along Drumul Poiana Pietrei until you go over the railroad tracks and you'll come to an intersection with Strada Sculptorilor. At the intersection walk along the unnamed, unpaved road through some industrial buildings and it ends up at the monastery. Second way, take the buses to the Condax stop and walk up the street to the previously mentioned odd intersection.

Reference List

<u>Highgate</u>

1. Patient, D. (2016, November 26). *The Highgate Vampire returns: Horror sightings of 'floating figure' spark UK panic.* Retrieved from

   https://www.dailystar.co.uk/news/latest-news/564244/Highgate-Vampire-London-UK-panic-horror-ghost-paranormal-sightings-Dracula

2. Theunredacted. (2016, December 05). *The Highgate Vampire: Horror of the Dead.* Retrieved from

   https://theunredacted.com/the-highgate-vampire-horror-of-the-dead/

3. Meier, A. (2017). *Highgate Cemetery.* Retrieved from

   https://www.atlasobscura.com/places/highgate-cemetery

4. Jones, R. (2017). *Haunted Graveyards.* Retrieved from http://www.haunted-london.com/london-graveyards.html

The Black Horse

5. The Black Horse. (2018). *Home Page.* Retrieved from https://www.blackhorsepluckley.co.uk

6. Skelton, P. (2018, November 20) *Dover Kent Archives: Black Horse Pluckley.* Retrieved from http://www.dover-kent.com/2014-project/Black-Horse-Pluckley.html

7. Real British Ghosts. (2010). *Pluckley – Most Haunted Village in England.* Retrieved from http://www.real-british-ghosts.com/most-haunted-village.html

Saint Nicholas Church

8. Pluckley Parish Council. (2017). *St Nicholas' Church.*

    Retrieved from https://www.pluckley.net/village-life/st-

    nicholass-church/

The Dering Arms

9. Hare, S. (2013). *Haunted: The Dering Arms, Pluckley,*

    Kent. Retrieved from http://eerieplace.com/haunted-

    dering-arms-pluckley/

The Dering Woods

10. TheComboser. (2015). *The Dering Wood Massacre.*

    Retrieved from

    https://www.reddit.com/r/nosleep/comments/2siqqf/t

    he_dering_wood_massacre/?st=jbpjoe1k&sh=16ee426

    d

11. The Ghost Hunt UK. (2017). *UK's Most Haunted – The*

    Screaming Woods. Retrieved from

http://theghosthuntuk.com/uks-haunted-screaming-woods/

Brighton

12. Wikipedia. (2018, April 24). *Henry Solomon.* Retrieved from https://en.wikipedia.org/wiki/Henry_Solomon

13. McDermott, W. (2018). *8 Most Haunted Places in Brighton.* Retrieved from https://www.hauntedrooms.co.uk/8-most-haunted-places-in-brighton

Houska Castle

14. Stonoceno. (2018). *Houska Castle.* Retrieved from https://www.atlasobscura.com/places/houska-castle

15. Wikipedia. (2018, October 17). *Houska Castle.* Retrieved from https://en.wikipedia.org/wiki/Houska_Castle

<u>Sedlec Ossuary</u>

16. Enemark, M. (2018). *Sedlec Ossuary "Bone Church."*

    Retrieved from

    https://www.atlasobscura.com/places/sedlec-ossuary

17. Wikipedia. (2017, July 28). *Sedlec Ossuary.* Retrieved

    from https://en.wikipedia.org/wiki/Sedlec_Ossuary

<u>Church of Saint Cyril & Methodus</u>

18. Wikipedia. (2018, December 27). *Reinhard Heydrich.*

    Retrieved from

    https://en.wikipedia.org/wiki/Reinhard_Heydrich

19. Wikipedia. (2018, December 21). *Operation*

    Anthropoid. Retrieved from

    https://en.wikipedia.org/wiki/Operation_Anthropoid

<u>Old Jewish Cemetery</u>

20. Biboul. (2018). *Old Jewish Cemetery.* Retrieved from

https://www.atlasobscura.com/places/old-jewish-

cemetery-1

21. Arbel, I. (2000, February 19). *Rabbi Loeb and the

Golem of Prague.* Retrieved from

https://pantheon.org/articles/l/loeb.html

Charles Bridge

22. Prag Way Tours. (2018). *The Ghost Child of Charles

Bridge Legend.* Retrieved from

https://pragueonsegway.com/ghost-child-charles-

bridge-legend/

23. Kralovska Cesta. (2018). *Charles Bridge.* Retrieved

from

http://www.kralovskacesta.cz/en/tour/objects/charles-

bridge_1.html

24. Naillon, E. (2018). *27 Noblemen Executed.* Retrieved

from https://www.private-prague-

guide.com/article/27-noblemen-executed/

<u>Hrad Cachtice</u>

25. Wikipedia. (2018, December 20). *Cachtice Castle.*

Retrieved from

https://en.wikipedia.org/wiki/Čachtice_Castle

26. A&E Television Network. (2009, November 13).

Bathory's Torturous Escapades are Exposed. Retrieved

from https://www.history.com/this-day-in-

history/bathorys-torturous-escapades-are-exposed

27. F. L. (2018). *Top 5 Medieval Castles in Slovakia that

have spooky legends hiding in them.* Retrieved from

https://www.slavorum.org/top-5-medieval-castles-in-

slovakia-that-have-spooky-legends-hiding-in-them/

Bridge of Lies

28. Poteaca, E. (2018, April). *The Legends Behind Sibiu's Bridge of Lies.* Retrieved from https://www.itinari.com/the-legends-behind-sibiu-s-bridge-of-lies-rkjd

Poenari Citadel

29. Serflac. (2018). *Poenari Castle.* Retrieved from https://www.atlasobscura.com/places/poenari-castle-vlad-the-impaler

Fortress of Targoviste and the Chindia Tower

30. Wikipedia. (2018, July 28). *Chindia Tower.* Retrieved from https://en.wikipedia.org/wiki/Chindia_Tower

31. Miller, E. (2005). *Vlad The Impaler: Breif History.* Retrieved from http://www.ucs.mun.ca/~emiller/vlad.html

<u>Hoia-Baciu Forest</u>

32. Haunted Forest. (2018). *Haunted Forest – Hoia-Baciu Forest.* Retrieved from https://hoiabaciuforest.com

33. Buchan, S. (2017, October 30). *Hoia Baciu: Inside The Creepiest Forest In Transylvania.* Retrieved from https://www.independent.co.uk/travel/europe/hoia-baciu-transylvania-haunted-trees-ufo-ghosts-how-to-visit-camping-alex-surducan-marius-a8023136.html

34. Museum of the Weird. (2014, July 07). *The Haunted, Alien Hotspot, Dimensional Portal Forest of Hoia-Baciu.* Retrieved from https://www.museumoftheweird.com/2014/07/07/the-haunted-alien-hotspot-dimensional-portal-forest-of-hoia-baciu/

<u>Chimopar Chemical Plant</u>

35. Casmirovici, R. (2018). *Chimopar: A gun powder factory damaged more than once.* Retrieved from

http://www.totallylost.eu/space/chimopar/

36. Travel Blog Europe. (2017). *Abandoed Chemical Factory With Deaths And Ruins.* Retrieved from

https://travelblogeurope.com/abandoned-chemical-factory-deaths-ruins/

Chiajna Monastery

37. Wikipedia. (2018, November 23). *Chiajna Monastery.* Retrieved from

https://en.wikipedia.org/wiki/Chiajna_Monastery

38. Alexandru. (2017, September 17). *Caragea's Plague.* Retrieved from

http://www.darksideofhistory.com/diseases-natural-disasters/carageas-plague/

39. Global Urban Legends. (2015, October 27). *Chiajna Monastery*. Retrieved from

http://globalurbanlegends.blogspot.com/2015/10/chiaj

na-monastery.html

40. About Eastern Europe. (2016, June 6). *Chiajna Monastery, A Mystery Remain Of The Middle Ages (Manastirea Chiajna).* Retrieved from http://about-eastern-europe.com/chiajna-monastery-a-mystery-remain-of-the-middle-ages-manastirea-chiajna/

Man: So say me, noble stranger, what brings you here this night?

[Death:] I have come to release you from the bitter taste of life.

[Man:] Why me? Why now? It cannot be my time. In youth am I still, and in flesh am I strong.

[Death:] And I have a disease for every sin that you have done.

[Man:] But I've done nothing wrong, nothing bad or untrue.

[Death:] Neither God nor Devil agrees with you!

Notes